To Mrs. Metcalf:
May you always
remember how
treasured you
are by the
ones whose lives
you touch each
day! Dara Witte

This book belongs to:

....

For Tyler, Eli and Olivia:

May you always remember
how very loved you are.
XOXO -Mommy

First Edition

ISBN: 978-0-578-49895-9 (hardcover)

This book is 100% independent and self-published.

My Love is Forever

Dara M. Witte

Illustrated by Celeste Villanueva

I dreamed of you before you came to be,

and I wondered what things you would DO, you would SEE.

Would you Dance gracefully?

Would you seek out adventure...

and sail the high seas?

Then, I prayed a prayer full of **blessings** and **love**,
that your destiny's path would reach ever above...

All you could **wish** for,
your heart's biggest **dream**...

That you **conquer** life's giants, however extreme.

And now that I look at you here in my arms,
I'm amazed by each detail, your smile and charms.

I see the whole world when I look at you,
and I know there is nothing that you cannot do.

You're here now beside me, though not long you'll stay. You'll **grow**. You'll **change**, and you'll **find** your own way.

So... always be **gentle**; treat all things with **care**.

When making decisions, please, always be fair.

Always show kindness and give second chances.
Believe in yourself and ignore sideways glances.

Do what is RIGHT,
and you'll never go wrong.

Always remember how **treasured** you are.
If you feel lonely, I'm **never** too far.
There's **never** a battle that you'll fight alone,
whether you're **near** me, or miles from home.

Like twinkling stars that shine up in the sky,
My Love is Forever, my dears, this is why...

I'm close as a **heartbeat**.
I'm **always** right here,

To **love** and to **guide** you until the storms clear.

You're my heart
and my sunshine.
You're my everything.

And though we don't know what the future may bring...
I'm **certain** that one thing, **my darlings**, is **true**:

The End

CPSIA information can be obtained at www.ICGtesting.com
Printed in the USA
LVIW010225240619
622129LV00002B/3